The Night of Christmas Eve

By

Nikolai Gogol

British Library Cataloguing-in-Publication Data
A catalogue record for this book is available from the
British Library

Nikolai Gogol

Nikolai Vasilievich Gogol was born in Sorochintsi, Ukraine in 1809. He attended the Poltava boarding school, and then the Nehzin high school, where he wrote for the school's literary journal and acted in theatrical productions. In 1828, after leaving school, Gogol moved to St. Petersburg with the ambition of becoming a professional author. At his own expense, he published a long Romantic poem. It was universally derided, and Gogol bought and destroyed all the copies, swearing never to write poetry again.

In 1831, Gogol brought out the first volume of his Ukrainian stories, *Evenings on a Farm Near Dikanka*. It met with immediate success, and he followed it a year later with a second volume. Around this time, Gogol met the great Russian poet Aleksandr Pushkin, with whom he developed a close friendship. Over the next decade or so, he worked with great industry, producing a great amount of short stories. Of these, 'The Nose' is regarded as a masterwork of comic short fiction, and 'The Overcoat' is now seen as one of the greatest short stories ever written; some years later, Dostoyevsky famously stated "We all come out from Gogol's 'Overcoat'." He also published *Dead Souls* (1842), a satirisation of serfdom, seen by many critics as the first 'modern' Russian novel and his greatest longer work.

Gogol spent time living abroad in later life, settling in Rome and developing a passion for opera. As he got older, criticism of his work began to drain him, and he turned to religion, making a pilgrimage to Jerusalem in 1848. Upon his return to Russia, under the encouragement of the fanatical priest, Father Konstantinovskii, Gogol subjected himself to a fatal course of fasting. He died in Moscow in 1852, aged 42. He is seen by many contemporary critics as one of the greatest short story writers who has ever lived, and the Father of Russia's Golden Age of Realism.

THE NIGHT OF CHRISTMAS EVE

A Legend of Little Russia

T H E last day before Christmas had just closed. A bright winter night had come on, stars had appeared, and the moon rose majestically in the heavens to shine upon good men and the whole of the world, so that they might gaily sing carols and hymns in praise of the nativity of Christ. The frost had grown more severe than during the day; but, to make up for this, everything had become so still that the crisping of the snow under-foot might be heard nearly half a verst round. As yet there was not a single group of young peasants to be seen under the windows of the cottages; the moon alone peeped stealthily in at them, as if inviting the maidens, who were decking themselves, to make haste and have a run on the crisp snow. Suddenly, out of the chimney of one of the cottages, volumes of smoke ascended in clouds towards the heavens, and in the midst of those clouds rose, on a besom, a witch.

If at that time the magistrate of Sorochinsk[1] had happened to pass in his carriage, drawn by three horses, his head covered by a lancer cap with sheepskin trimming, and wrapped in his great cloak, covered with blue cloth and lined with black sheepskin, and with his tightly plaited lash, which he uses for making the driver drive faster—if this worthy gentleman had happened to pass at that time, no doubt he would have seen the witch, because there is no witch who could glide away without his seeing her. He knows to a certainty how many sucking pigs each swine brings forth in each cottage, how much linen lies in each box, and what each one has pawned in the brandy-shop out of his clothes

---

[1] Chief town of a district in the government of Poltava.

or his household furniture. But the magistrate of Sorochinsk happened *not* to pass; and then, what has he to do with those out of his jurisdiction? he has his own circuit. And the witch by this time had risen so high that she only looked like a little dark spot up above; but wherever that spot went, one star after another disappeared from heaven. In a short time the witch had got a whole sleeveful of them. Some three or four only remained shining. On a sudden, from the opposite side, appeared another spot, which went on growing, spreading, and soon became no longer a spot. A short-sighted man, had he put, not only spectacles, but even the wheels of a britzka on his nose, would never have been able to make out what it was. In front, it was just like a German;[1] a narrow snout, incessantly turning on every side, and smelling about, ended like those of our pigs, in a small, round, flattened end; its legs were so thin, that had the village elder got no better, he would have broken them to pieces in the first squatting-dance. But, as if to make amends for these deficiencies, it might have been taken, viewed from behind, for the provincial advocate, so much was its long pointed tail like the skirt of our dress-coats. And yet, a look at the goat's beard under its snout, at the small horns sticking out of its head, and at the whole of its figure, which was no whiter than that of a chimney-sweep, would have sufficed to make anyone guess that it was neither a German nor a provincial advocate, but the devil in person, to whom only one night more was left for walking about the world and tempting good men to sin. On the morrow, at the first stroke of the church bell, he was to run, with his tail between his legs, back to his quarters. The devil then, and the devil it was, stole warily to the moon, and stretched out his hand to get hold of it; but at the very same moment he drew it hastily back again, as if he had burnt it, shook his foot, sucked his fingers, ran round on the

---

[1] Every foreigner, whatever may be his station, used to be called a German by Russian peasants. A dress coat was often sufficient to procure this name for its wearer.

other side, sprang at the moon once more, and once more drew his hand away. Still, notwithstanding his being baffled, the cunning devil did not desist from his mischievous designs. Dashing desperately forwards, he grasped the moon with both hands, and, making wry faces and blowing hard, he threw it from one hand to the other, like a peasant who has taken a live coal in his hand to light his pipe. At last, he hastily hid it in his pocket, and went on his way as if nothing had happened.

At Dikanka,[1] nobody suspected that the devil had stolen the moon. It is true that the village scribe, coming out of the brandy-shop on all fours, saw how the moon, without any apparent reason, danced in the sky, and took his oath of it before the whole village, but the distrustful villagers shook their heads, and even laughed at him. And now, what was the reason that the devil had decided on such an unlawful step? Simply this: he knew very well that the rich Cossack Choop[2] was invited to an evening party at the parish clerk's, where he was to meet the elder, also a relation of the clerk, who was in the archbishop's chapel, and who wore a blue coat and had a most sonorous *basso profondo*, the Cossack Sverbygooze, and some other acquaintances; where there would be for supper, not only the *kootia*,[3] but also a *varenookha*,[4] as well as corn-brandy, flavoured with saffron, and divers other dainties. He knew that in the meantime Choop's daughter, the belle of the village, would remain at home; and he knew, moreover, that to this daughter would come the blacksmith, a lad of athletic strength, whom the devil

[1] A village in the government of Poltava, in which Gogol placed the scene of most of his folk stories.

[2] Almost every family name in Little Russia has some meaning; the name of *Choop* means the tuft of hair growing on the crown of the head, which was alone left to grow by the Little Russians; they uniformly shaved the occiput and temples; in Great or Middle Russia, peasants, on the contrary, let the hair grow on these parts. Now there is not much difference in headdress.

[3] *Kootia* is a dish of boiled rice and plums, eaten by Russians on Christmas Eve.

[4] *Varenookha* is corn-brandy boiled with fruit and spice.

held in greater aversion than even the sermons of Father Kondrat. When the blacksmith had no work on hand he used to practise painting, and had acquired the reputation of being the best painter in the whole district. Even the centurion[1] had expressly sent for him to Poltava, for the purpose of painting the wooden palisade round his house. All the tureens out of which the Cossacks of Dikanka ate their *borsch* were adorned with the paintings of the blacksmith. He was a man of great piety, and often painted images of the saints; even now, some of them may be seen in the village church; but his masterpiece was a painting on the right side of the church-door; in it he had represented the Apostle Peter, at the Day of Judgment, with the keys in his hand, driving an evil spirit out of hell; the terrified devil, apprehending his ruin, rushed hither and thither, and the sinners, freed from their imprisonment, pursued and thrashed him with scourges, logs of wood, and anything that came to hand. All the time that the blacksmith was busy with this picture, and was painting it on a great board, the devil used all his endeavours to spoil it; he pushed his hand, raised the ashes out of the forge, and spread them over the painting; but, notwithstanding all this, the work was finished, the board was brought to the church, and fixed in the wall of the porch. From that time the devil vowed vengeance on the blacksmith. He had only one night left to roam about the world, but even in that night he sought to play some evil trick upon the blacksmith. For this reason he had resolved to steal the moon, for he knew that old Choop was lazy above all things, not quick to stir his feet; that the road to the clerk's was long, and went across back lanes, next to mills, along the churchyard, and over the top of a precipice; and though the *varenookha* and the saffron brandy might have got the better of Choop's laziness on a moonlight night, yet, in such darkness, it would be difficult to suppose that anything could

[1] A rank in irregular troops, corresponding to that of captain in the army.

prevail on him to get down from his oven[1] and quit his cottage. And the blacksmith, who had long been at variance with Choop, would not on any account, in spite even of his strength, visit his daughter in his presence.

So stood events: hardly had the devil hidden the moon in his pocket, when all at once it grew so dark that many could not have found their way to the brandy-shop, still less to the clerk's. The witch, finding herself suddenly in darkness, shrieked aloud. The devil coming near her, took her hand, and began to whisper to her those same things which are usually whispered to all womankind.

How oddly things go on in this world of ours! Everyone who lives in it endeavours to copy and ape his neighbour. Of yore there was nobody at Mirgorod[2] but the judge and the mayor, who in winter wore fur cloaks covered with cloth; all their subordinates went in plain uncovered *too-loops*;[3] and now, only see, the deputy, as well as the under-cashier, wear new cloaks of black sheep fur covered with cloth. Two years ago, the village scribe and the town clerk bought blue nankeen, for which they paid full sixty kopecks the *arsheen*. The sexton, too, has found it necessary to have nankeen trousers for the summer, and a striped woollen waistcoat. In short, there is no one who does not try to cut a figure. When will the time come when men will desist from vanity? One may wager that many will be astonished at finding the devil making love. The most provoking part of it is, to think that really he fancies himself a beau, when the fact is, that he has such a phiz that one is ashamed to look at it—such a phiz that, as one of my friends says, it is the abomination of abominations; and yet he, too, ventures to make love!

But it grew so dark in the sky, and under the sky, that there

[1] The ovens of the peasants' cottages are built in the shape of furnaces, with a place on the top which is reserved for sleeping.

[2] Chief town of a district in the government of Poltava.

[3] Long coats made of sheepskins, with the fur worn inside. They are used in Russia by common people.

was no possibility of further seeing what passed between the devil and the witch.

"So thou sayest, kinsman, that thou hast not yet been in the clerk's new abode?" said the Cossack Choop, stepping out of his cottage, to a tall meagre peasant in a short *tooloop*, with a well-grown beard, which it was evident had remained at least a fortnight untouched by the piece of scythe which the peasants use instead of a razor.[1] "There will be a good drinking party," continued Choop, endeavouring to smile at these words, "only we must not be too late;" and with this, Choop drew still closer his belt, which was tightly girded round his *tooloop*, pulled his cap over his eyes, and grasped more firmly his whip, the terror of importunate dogs; but looking up, remained fixed to the spot. "What the devil! look, kinsman!"

"What now?" uttered the kinsman, also lifting up his head.

"What now? Why, where is the moon gone?"

"Ah! sure enough, gone she is."

"Yes, that she is!" said Choop, somewhat cross at the equanimity of the kinsman, "and it's all the same to thee."

"And how could I help it?"

"That must be the trick of some evil spirit," continued Choop, rubbing his moustaches with his sleeve. "Wretched dog, may he find no glass of brandy in the morning! Just as if it were to laugh at us; and I was purposely looking out of window as I was sitting in the room; such a splendid night; so light, the snow shining so brightly in the moonlight; everything to be seen as if by day; and now we have hardly crossed the threshold, and behold it is as dark as blindness!"

And Choop continued a long time in the same strain, moaning and groaning, and thinking all the while what was to be done. He greatly wished to have a gossip about all sorts of nonsense at the clerk's lodgings, where, he felt quite sure, were already assembled the elder, the newly-arrived *basso profondo*, as well as the tar-maker Nikita, who went every

[1] Little Russians shave beard and whiskers, leaving only their moustaches.

fortnight, to Poltava on business, and who told such funny stories that his hearers used to laugh till they were obliged to hold their belts. Choop even saw, in his mind's eye, the *varenookha* brought forth upon the table. All this was most enticing, it is true; but then the darkness of the night put him in mind of the laziness which is so very dear to every Cossack. Would it not be well now to lie upon the oven, with his feet drawn up to his body, quietly enjoying a pipe, and listening through a delightful drowsiness to the songs and carols of the gay lads and maidens who would come in crowds under the windows? Were Choop alone, there is no doubt he would have preferred the latter; but to go in company would not be so tedious or so frightful after all, be the night ever so dark; besides, he did not choose to appear to another either lazy or timorous; so, putting an end to his grumbling, he once more turned to the kinsman. "Well, kinsman; so the moon is gone?"

"She is."

"Really, it is very strange! Give me a pinch of thy snuff. Beautiful snuff it is; where dost thou buy it, kinsman?"

"I should like to know what is so beautiful in it," answered the kinsman, shutting his snuff-box, made of birch bark and adorned with different designs pricked on it; "it would not make an old hen sneeze."

"I remember," continued Choop in the same strain, "the defunct pot-house keeper, Zoozooha, once brought me some snuff from Niegen.[1] That was what I call snuff—capital snuff! Well, kinsman, what are we to do? The night is dark."

"Well, I am ready to remain at home;" answered the kinsman, taking hold of the handle of the door.

Had not the kinsman spoken thus, Choop would certainly have remained at home; but now, there was something which prompted him to do quite the contrary. "No, kinsman; we will go; go we must;" and whilst saying this, he was already cross with himself for having thus spoken. He

[1] Chief town of a district in the government of Chernigoff.

7

was much displeased at having to walk so far on such a night, and yet he felt gratified at having had his own way, and having gone contrary to the advice he had received. The kinsman, without the least expression of discontent on his face, like a man perfectly indifferent to sitting at home or to taking a walk, looked round, scratched his shoulder with the handle of his cudgel, and away went the two kinsmen.

Let us now take a glance at what Choop's beautiful daughter was about when left alone. Oxana has not yet completed her seventeenth year, and already all the people of Dikanka, nay, even the people beyond it, talk of nothing but her beauty. The young men are unanimous in their decision, and have proclaimed her the most beautiful girl that ever was, or ever can be, in the village. Oxana knows this well, and hears everything that is said about her, and she is, of course, as capricious as a beauty knows how to be. Had she been born to wear a lady's elegant dress, instead of a simple peasant's petticoat and apron, she would doubtless have proved so fine a lady that no maid could have remained in her service. The lads followed her in crowds; but she used to put their patience to such trials, that they all ended by leaving her to herself, and taking up with other girls, not so spoiled as she was. The blacksmith was the only one who did not desist from his love suit, but continued it, notwithstanding her ill-treatment, in which he had no less share than the others.

When her father was gone, Oxana remained for a long time ornamenting herself, and coquetting before a small looking-glass, framed in tin. She could not tire of admiring her own likeness in the glass. "Why do men talk so much about my being so pretty?" said she, absently, merely for the sake of gossiping aloud. "Nonsense; there is nothing pretty in me." But the mirror, reflecting her fresh, animated, childish features, with brilliant dark eyes, and a smile most inexpressibly bewitching, proved quite the contrary. "Unless," continued

4

the beauty, holding up the mirror, "maybe, my black eyebrows and my dark eyes are so pretty that no prettier are to be found in the world; as for this little snub nose of mine, and my cheeks and my lips, what is there pretty in them? or, are my tresses so very beautiful? Oh! one might be frightened at them in the dark; they seem like so many serpents twining round my head. No, I see very well that I am not at all beautiful!" And then, on a sudden, holding the looking-glass a little further off, "No," she exclaimed, exultingly, "no, I really am pretty! and how pretty! how beautiful! What joy shall I bring to him whose wife I am to be! How delighted will my husband be to look at me! He will forget all other thoughts in his love for me! He will smother me with kisses."

"A strange girl, indeed," muttered the blacksmith, who had in the meantime entered the room, "and no small share of vanity has she got! There she stands for the last hour, looking at herself in the glass, and cannot leave off, and moreover praises herself aloud."

"Yes, indeed, lads! is anyone of you a match for me?" continued the pretty flirt; "look at me, how gracefully I walk; my bodice is embroidered with red silk, and what ribbons I have got for my hair! You have never seen any to be compared with them! All this my father has bought on purpose, that I may marry the smartest fellow that ever was born!" and so saying, she laughingly turned round and saw the blacksmith. She uttered a cry and put on a severe look, standing erect before him. The blacksmith was quite abashed. It would be difficult to specify the expression of the strange girl's somewhat sunburnt face; there was a degree of severity in it, and, in this same severity, somewhat of raillery at the blacksmith's bashfulness, as well as a little vexation, which spread an almost imperceptible blush over her features. All this was so complicated, and became her so admirably well, that the best thing to have done would have been to give her thousands and thousands of kisses.

"Why didst thou come hither?" she began. "Dost thou wish me to take up the shovel and drive thee from the house? Oh! you, all of you, know well how to insinuate yourselves into our company! You scent out in no time when the father has turned his back on the house. Oh! I know you well! Is my box finished?"

"It will be ready; dear heart of mine—it will be ready after the festival. Couldst thou but know how much trouble it has cost me—two whole nights I worked on it. Sure enough, thou wilt find no such box anywhere; not even belonging to a priest's wife. The iron I used for binding it! I did not use the like even for the centurion's dog-cart. And then, the painting of it! Wert thou to go on thy white feet round all the district, thou wouldst not find such another painting. The whole of the box will sparkle with red and blue flowers. It will be a delight to look upon. Be not angry with me. Allow me—be it only to speak to thee—nay, even to look on thee."

"Who means to forbid it? Speak and look," and she sat down on the bench, threw one more glance at the glass, and began to adjust the plaits on her head, looked at her neck, at her new bodice, embroidered with silk, and a scarcely visible expression of self-content played over her lips and cheeks and brightened her eyes.

"Allow me to sit down beside thee," said the blacksmith.

"Be seated," answered Oxana, preserving the same expression about her mouth and in her looks.

"Beautiful Oxana! Nobody will ever have done looking at thee—let me kiss thee!" exclaimed the blacksmith, recovering his presence of mind, and drawing her towards him, endeavoured to snatch a kiss; her cheek was already quite close to the blacksmith's lips, when Oxana sprang aside and pushed him back. "What wilt thou want next? When he has got honey, he wants a spoon too. Away with thee! thy hands are harder than iron, and thou smellest of smoke thyself; I really think thou hast besmeared me with thy soot." She then took the mirror and once more began to adorn herself.

"She does not care for me," thought the blacksmith, hanging down his head. "Everything is but play to her, and I am here like a fool standing before her, and never taking my eyes off her. Charming girl. What would I not do only to know what is passing in her heart. Whom does she love? But no, she cares for no one, she is fond only of herself, she delights in the sufferings she causes to my own poor self, and my grief prevents me from thinking of anything else, and I love her as nobody in the world ever loved or is likely to love."

"Is it true that thy mother is a witch?" asked Oxana, laughing; and the blacksmith felt as if everything within him laughed too, as if that laugh had found an echo in his heart and in all his veins; and at the same time he felt provoked at having no right to cover her pretty laughing face with kisses.

"What do I care about my mother! Thou art my mother, my father—all that I hold precious in the world! Should the Tsar send for me to his presence and say to me, 'Blacksmith Vakoola, ask of me whatever I have best in my realm—I'll give it all to thee; I'll order to have made for thee a golden smithy, where thou shalt forge with silver hammers.' 'I'll none of it,' would I answer the Tsar. 'I'll have no precious stones, no golden smithy, no, not even the whole of thy realm—give me only my Oxana!'"

"Now, only see what a man thou art! But my father has got another idea in his head; thou'lt see if he does not marry thy mother!"[1] said Oxana with an arch smile. "But what can it mean? Why haven't the girls come—it is high time for our carol. I am getting dull."

"Never mind about them, my beauty!"

"But, of course, I do mind; they will bring some lads with them, and then, how merry we shall be! I can fancy all the droll stories that will be told!"

"So thou art merry with them?"

---

[1] This, according to the laws of the Greek Church, would prevent their children from intermarrying.

"Of course, merrier than with thee. Ah! there is somebody knocking at the door; it must be the girls and the lads!"

"Why need I stay any longer?" thought the blacksmith. "She laughs at me; she cares no more about me than about a rust-eaten horseshoe. But, be it so. I will at least give no one an opportunity to laugh at me. Let me only mark who it is she prefers to me. I'll teach him how to——"

His meditation was cut short by a loud knocking at the door, and a harsh, "Open the door," rendered still harsher by the frost.

"Be quiet, I'll go and open it myself," said the blacksmith, stepping into the passage with the firm intention of giving vent to his wrath by breaking the bones of the first man who should come in his way.

The frost increased, and it became so cold that the devil went hopping from one hoof to the other, and blowing his fingers to warm his benumbed hands. And, of course, he could not feel otherwise than quite frozen; all day long he did nothing but saunter about hell, where, as everybody knows, it is by no means so cold as in our winter air; and where, with his cap on his head, and standing before a furnace as if really a cook, he felt as much pleasure in roasting sinners as a peasant's wife feels at frying sausages for Christmas. The witch, though warmly clad, felt cold too, so lifting up her arms, and putting one foot before the other, just as if she were skating, without moving a limb, she slid down as if from a sloping ice mountain right into the chimney. The devil followed her example; but as the devil is swifter than any boot-wearing beau, it is not at all astonishing that at the very entrance of the chimney he went down upon the shoulders of the witch, and both slipped down together into a wide oven, with pots all round it. The lady traveller first of all noiselessly opened the oven-door a little, to see if her son Vakoola had not brought home some party of friends; but there being nobody in the room, and only some sacks lying in the middle of it on the floor, she crept out of the oven, took off her warm coat, put her dress in order, and was quite tidy in no time, so that nobody could ever possibly have suspected her of having ridden on a besom a minute before.

The mother of the blacksmith Vakoola was about forty; she was neither handsome nor plain; indeed it is difficult to be handsome at that age. Yet, she knew well how to make herself pleasant to the aged Cossacks (who, by the bye, did not care much about a handsome face); many went to call upon her, the elder, Ossip Nikiphorovitch the clerk (of course when his wife was from home), the Cossack Kornius Choop, the Cossack Kassian Sverbygooze. At all events this must be said for her, she perfectly well understood how to manage them; none of them ever suspected for a moment that he had a rival. Was a pious peasant going home from church on some holiday; or was a Cossack, in bad weather, on his way to the vodka-shop; what should prevent him from paying Solokha a visit, to eat some greasy curd dumplings with sour cream, and to have a gossip with the talkative and good-natured mistress of the cottage? And the Cossack made a long circuit on his way to the vodka-shop, and called it "just looking in as he passed." When Solokha went to church on a holiday, she always wore a gay-coloured petticoat, with another short blue one over it, adorned with two gold braids, sewed on behind it in the shape of two curly moustaches. When she took her place at the right side of the church, the clerk was sure to cough and wink at her; the elder twirled his moustaches, twisted his crown-lock of hair round his ear, and said to his neighbour, "A splendid woman! a devilish fine woman!" Solokha nodded to everyone, and everyone thought that Solokha nodded to him alone. But those who liked to pry into other people's business, noticed that Solokha exerted the utmost of her civility towards the Cossack Choop.

Choop was a widower; eight ricks of corn stood always

before his cottage; two strong bulls used to put their heads out of their wattled shed, gaze up and down the street, and bellow every time they caught a glimpse of their cousin a cow, or their uncle the stout ox; the bearded goat climbed up to the very roof, and bleated from thence in a key as shrill as that of the mayor, and teased the turkeys which were proudly walking in the yard, and turned his back as soon as he saw his inveterate enemies, the urchins, who used to laugh at his beard. In Choop's boxes there was plenty of linen, many warm coats, and many old-fashioned dresses bound with gold braid; for his late wife had been a dashing woman. Every year there was a couple of beds planted with tobacco in his kitchen-garden, which was, besides, well provided with poppies, cabbages and sunflowers. All this, Solokha thought, would suit very well if united to her own household; she was already mentally regulating the management of this property when it should pass into her hands; and so she went on increasing in kindness towards old Choop. At the same time, to prevent her son Vakoola from making an impression on Choop's daughter, and getting the whole of the property (in which case she was sure of not being allowed to interfere with anything), she had recourse to the usual means of all women of her age—she took every opportunity to make Choop quarrel with the blacksmith. These very artifices were perhaps the cause that it came to be rumoured amongst the old women (particularly when they happened to take a drop too much at some gay party) that Solokha was positively a witch; that young Kiziakaloopenko had seen on her back a tail no bigger than a common spindle; that on the last Thursday but one she ran across the road in the shape of a black kitten; that once there had come to the priest a hog, which crowed like a cock, put on Father Kondrat's hat, and then ran away. It so happened that as the old women were discussing this point, there came by Tymish Korostiavoï, the herdsman. He could not help telling how, last summer, just before St. Peter's fast, as he laid himself down for sleep in his shed, and had put some straw under his head, with his own eyes he beheld the witch, with her hair unplaited and nothing on but her shift, come and milk her cows; how he was so bewitched that he could not move any of his limbs; how she came to him and greased his lips with some nasty stuff, so that he could not help spitting all the next day. And yet all these stories seem of a somewhat doubtful character, because there is nobody but the magistrate of Sorochinsk who can distinguish a witch. This was the reason why all the chief Cossacks waved their hands on hearing such stories. "Mere nonsense, stupid hags!" was their usual answer.

Having come out of the oven and put herself to rights, Solokha, like a good housewife, began to arrange and put everything in its place; but she did not touch the sacks: "Vakoola had brought them in—he might take them out again." In the meantime the devil, as he was coming down the chimney, caught a glimpse of Choop, who, arm in arm with his kinsman, was already a long way off from his cottage. Instantly, the devil flew out of the chimney, ran across the way, and began to break asunder the heaps of frozen snow which were lying all around. Then began a snow-storm. The air was all whitened with snow-flakes. The snow went rushing backwards and forwards, and threatened to cover, as it were with a net, the eyes, mouth and ears of the pedestrians. Then the devil flew into the chimney once more, quite sure that both kinsmen would retrace their steps to Choop's house, who would find there the blacksmith, and give him so sound a thrashing that the latter would never again have the strength to take a brush in his hand and paint offensive caricatures.

As soon as the snow-storm began, and the wind blew sharply in his eyes, Choop felt some remorse, and, pulling his cap over his very eyes, he began to abuse himself, the devil and his own kinsman. Yet his vexation was but assumed; the snow-storm was rather welcome to Choop. The distance they had still to go before reaching the dwelling of the clerk was eight times as long as that which they had already gone; so they turned back. They now had the wind behind them; but nothing could be seen through the whirling snow.

"Stop, kinsman, it seems to me that we have lost our way," said Choop, after having gone a little distance. "There is not a single cottage to be seen! Ah! what a storm it is! Go a little on that side, kinsman, and see if thou canst not find the road; and I will seek it on this side. Who but the devil would ever have persuaded anyone to leave the house in such a storm! Don't forget, kinsman, to call me when thou findest the road. Eh! what a lot of snow the devil has sent into my eyes!"

But the road was not to be found. The kinsman, in his long boots, started off on one side, and, after having rambled backwards and forwards, ended by finding his way right into the vodka-shop. He was so glad of it that he forgot everything else, and, after shaking off the snow, stepped into the passage without once thinking about his kinsman who had remained in the snow. Choop in the meantime fancied he had found out the road; he stopped and began to shout with all the strength of his lungs, but seeing that his kinsman did not come, he decided on proceeding alone.

In a short time he saw his cottage. Great heaps of snow lay around it and covered its roof. Rubbing his hands, which were numbed by the frost, he began to knock at the door, and in a loud tone ordered his daughter to open it.

"What dost thou want?" roughly demanded the blacksmith, stepping out.

Choop, on recognising the blacksmith's voice, stepped a little aside. "No, surely this is not my cottage," said he to himself; "the blacksmith would not come to my cottage. And yet—now I look at it again, it cannot be his. Whose, then, can it be? Ah! how came I not to know it at once! it is the cottage of lame Levchenko, who has lately married a young wife; his is the only one like mine. That is the reason why it seemed so strange to me that I got home so soon. But, let me see, why is the blacksmith here? Levchenko, as far as I know, is now sitting at the clerk's. Eh! he! he! he! the blacksmith comes to see his young wife! That's what it is! Well, now I see it all!"

"Who art thou? and what hast thou to do lurking about this door?" asked the blacksmith, in a still harsher voice, and coming nearer.

"No," thought Choop, "I'll not tell him who I am; he might beat me, the cursed fellow!" and then, changing his voice, answered, "My good man, I come here in order to amuse you by singing carols beneath your window."

"Go to the devil with thy carols!" angrily cried Vakoola. "What dost thou wait for? didst thou hear me? begone, directly."

Choop himself had already the same prudent intention; but he felt cross at being obliged to obey the blacksmith's command. Some evil spirit seemed to prompt him to say something unpleasant to Vakoola.

"What makes thee shout in that way?" asked he in the same assumed voice; "my intention is to sing a carol, and that is all."

"Ah! words are not sufficient for thee!" and immediately after, Choop felt a heavy blow upon his shoulders.

"Now, I see, thou art getting quarrelsome!" said Choop, retreating a few paces.

"Begone, begone!" exclaimed the blacksmith, striking again.

"What now!" exclaimed Choop, in a voice which expressed at the same time pain, anger, and fear. "I see thou quarrellest in good earnest, and strikest hard."

"Begone, begone!" again exclaimed the blacksmith, and shut the door violently.

"Look, what a bully!" said Choop, once more alone in the street. "But thou hadst better not come near me! There's a man for you! giving thyself such airs, too! Dost thou think there is no one to bring thee to reason? I *will* go, my dear fellow, and to the police-officer will I go. I'll teach thee who I am! I care not for thy being blacksmith and painter. However, I must see to my back and shoulders: I think there are bruises on them. The devil's son strikes hard, it seems. It is a pity it's so cold, I cannot take off my fur coat. Stay a while, confounded blacksmith; may the devil break thy bones and thy smithy too! Take thy time—I will make thee dance, cursed squabbler! But, now I think of it, if he is not at home, Solokha must be alone. Hem! her dwelling is not far from here; shall I go? At this time nobody will trouble us. Perhaps I may. Ah! that cursed blacksmith, how he has beaten me!"

And Choop, rubbing his back, went in another direction. The pleasure which was in store for him in meeting Solokha diverted his thoughts from his pain, and made him quite insensible to the snow and ice, which, notwithstanding the whistling of the wind, might be heard crackling under his feet. Sometimes a half-benignant smile brightened his face, and his beard and moustaches were whitened over by snow with the same rapidity as that displayed by a barber who has tyrannically got hold of the nose of his victim. But for the snow which danced backwards and forwards before the eyes, Choop might have been seen a long time, stopping now and then to rub his back, muttering, "How painfully that cursed blacksmith has beaten me!" and then proceeding on his way.

At the time when the dashing gentleman, with a tail and a goat's beard, flew out of the chimney, and then into the chimney again, the pouch which hung by a shoulder-belt at his side, and in which he had hidden the stolen moon, in some way or other caught in something in the oven, flew open, and the moon, availing herself of the opportunity, mounted through the chinmey of Solokha's cottage and rose majestically in the sky. It grew light all at once; the storm subsided; the snow-covered fields seemed all covered with silver, set with crystal stars; even the frost seemed to have grown milder; crowds of lads and lasses made their appearance with sacks upon their shoulders; songs resounded, and but few cottagers were without a band of carollers. How beautifully the moon shines! It would be difficult to describe the charm one feels in sauntering on such a night among the troops of maidens who laugh and sing, and of lads who are ready to adopt every trick and invention suggested by the gay and smiling night. The tightly-belted fur coat is warm; the frost makes one's cheeks tingle more sharply; and the Cunning One, himself, seems, from behind your back, to urge you to all kinds of frolics. A crowd of maidens, with sacks, pushed their way into Choop's cottage, surrounded Oxana, and bewildered the blacksmith by their shouts, their laughter, and their stories. Everyone was in haste to tell something new to the beauty; some unloaded their sacks, and boasted of the quantity of loaves, sausages and curd dumplings which they had already received in reward for their carolling. Oxana seemed to be all pleasure and joy, went on chattering, first with one, then with another, and never for a moment ceased laughing. The blacksmith looked with anger and envy at her joy, and cursed the carolling, notwithstanding his having been mad about it himself in former times.

"Odarka," said the joyful beauty, turning to one of the girls, "thou hast got on new boots! Ah! how beautiful they are! all ornamented with gold too! Thou art happy, Odarka, to have a suitor who can make thee such presents; I have nobody who would give me such pretty boots!"

"Don't grieve about boots, my incomparable Oxana!" chimed in the blacksmith; "I will bring thee such boots as few ladies wear."

"Thou?" said Oxana, throwing a quick disdainful glance at him. "We shall see where thou wilt get such boots as will

suit my foot, unless thou bringest me the very boots which
the Tsarina wears!"

"Just see what she has taken a fancy to now!" shouted the
group of laughing girls.

"Yes!" haughtily continued the beauty, "I call all of you
to witness, that if the blacksmith Vakoola brings me the very
boots which the Tsarina wears, I pledge him my word
instantly to marry him."

The maidens led away the capricious belle.

"Laugh on, laugh on!" said the blacksmith, stepping out
after them. "I myself laugh at my own folly. It is in vain
that I think over and over again, where have I left my wits?
She does not love me—well, God be with her! Is Oxana the
only woman in all the world? Thanks be to God! there are
many handsome maidens in the village besides Oxana.
Yes, indeed, what is Oxana? No good housewife will ever
be made out of her; she only understands how to deck herself.
No, truly, it is high time for me to leave off making a fool of
myself." And yet at the very moment when he came to this
resolution, the blacksmith saw before his eyes the laughing
face of Oxana, teasing him with the words—"Bring me,
blacksmith, the Tsarina's own boots, and I will marry thee!"
He was all agitation, and his every thought was bent on
Oxana alone.

The carolling groups of lads on one side, of maidens on the
other, passed rapidly from street to street. But the blacksmith went on his way without noticing anything, and without taking any part in the rejoicings, in which, till now, he
had delighted above all others.

The devil had, in the meanwhile, quickly reached the
utmost limits of tenderness in his conversation with Solokha;
he kissed her hand with nearly the same look as the magistrate used when making love to the priest's wife; he pressed
his hand upon his heart, sighed, and told her that if she did
not choose to consider his passion, and meet it with due

return, he had made up his mind to throw himself into the water, and send his soul right down to hell. But Solokha was not so cruel—the more so, as the devil, it is well known, was in league with her. Moreover, she liked to have someone to flirt with, and rarely remained alone. This evening she expected to be without any visitor, on account of all the chief inhabitants of the village being invited to the clerk's house. And yet quite the contrary happened. Hardly had the devil set forth his demand, when the voice of the stout elder was heard. Solokha ran to open the door, and the quick devil crept into one of the sacks that were lying on the floor. The elder, after having shaken off the snow from his cap, and drunk a cup of vodka which Solokha presented to him, told her that he had not gone to the clerk's on account of the snow-storm, and that, having seen a light in her cottage, he had come to pass the evening with her. The elder had just done speaking when there was a knock at the door, and the clerk's voice was heard from without. "Hide me wherever thou wilt," whispered the elder; "I should not like to meet the clerk." Solokha could not at first conceive where so stout a visitor might possibly be hidden; at last she thought the biggest charcoal sack would be fit for the purpose; she threw the charcoal into a tub, and the sack being empty, in went the stout elder, moustaches, head, cap and all. Presently the clerk made his appearance, giving way to a short dry cough, and rubbing his hands together. He told her how none of his guests had come, and how he was heartily glad of it, as it had given him the opportunity of taking a walk to her abode, in spite of the snow-storm. After this he came a step nearer to her, coughed once more, laughed, touched her bare plump arm with his fingers, and said in a sly, and at the same time a pleased voice, "What have you got here, most magnificent Solokha?" after which words he jumped back a few steps.

"How, what? Ossip Nikiphorovitch! it is my arm!" answered Solokha.

"Hem! Your arm! he! he! he!" smirked the clerk, greatly rejoiced at his beginning, and he took a turn in the room.

"And what is this, dearest Solokha?" said he, with the same expression, again coming to her, gently touching her throat, and once more springing back.

"As if you cannot see for yourself, Ossip Nikiphorovitch!" answered Solokha, "it is my throat and my necklace on it."

"Hem! Your necklace upon your throat! he! he! he!" and again he walked up and down the room, rubbing his hands.

"And what have you here, unequalled Solokha?"

We know not what the clerk's long fingers would now have touched, if just at that moment he had not heard a knock at the door, and, at the same time, the voice of the Cossack Choop.

"Heavens! what an unwelcome visitor!" said the clerk in a fright, "whatever will happen if a person of my character is met here! If it should reach the ears of Father Kondrat!" But, in fact, the clerk's real anxiety was of quite a different description; above all things he dreaded lest his wife should be acquainted with his visit to Solokha; and he had good reason to dread her, for her powerful hand had already made his thick plait[1] a very thin one. "In Heaven's name, most virtuous Solokha!" said he, trembling all over; "your goodness, as the Scripture saith, in St. Luke, chapter the thir—thir—there is somebody knocking, decidedly there is somebody knocking at the door! In Heaven's name let me hide somewhere!"

Solokha threw the charcoal out of another sack into the tub, and in crept the clerk, who, being by no means corpulent, sat down at the very bottom of it, so that there would have

[1] Village clerks in Russia used to have their hair plaited. Many priests, not allowed by the custom of the land to cut their hair short, wore it, for convenience' sake, plaited when at home and only loosened it during the performance of the duties of their office. This is still the case.

been room enough to put more than half a sackful of charcoal on top of him.

"Good-evening, Solokha," said Choop, stepping into the room. "Thou didst not perhaps expect me, didst thou? Certainly not; may be I hindered thee," continued Choop, putting on a gay knowing look, which expressed at once that his lazy brain was at work, and that he was on the point of saying some sharp and sportive witticism. "Maybe thou wert already engaged in flirting with somebody! Maybe thou hast already hidden someone? Is it so?" said he; and delighted at his own wit, Choop gave way to a hearty laugh, inwardly exulting at the thought that he was the only one who enjoyed the favours of Solokha. "Well now, Solokha, give me a glass of vodka; I think the abominable frost has frozen my throat! What a night for a Christmas Eve! As it began snowing, Solokha—just listen, Solokha—as it began snowing —eh! I cannot move my hands; impossible to unbutton my coat! Well, as it began snowing——"

"Open!" cried someone in the street, at the same time giving a thump at the door.

"Somebody is knocking at the door!" said Choop, stopping in his speech.

"Open!" cried the voice, still louder.

"'Tis the blacksmith!" said Choop, taking his cap; "listen, Solokha!—put me wherever thou wilt! on no account in the world would I meet that confounded lad! Devil's son! I wish he had a blister as big as a haycock under each eye."

Solokha was so frightened that she rushed backwards and forwards in the room, and quite unconscious of what she did, shoved Choop into the same sack where the clerk was already sitting. The poor clerk had to restrain his cough and his sighs when the weighty Cossack sat down almost on his head, and placed his boots, covered with frozen snow, just on his temples.

The blacksmith came in, without saying a word, without

taking off his cap, and threw himself on the bench. It was easy to see that he was in a very bad temper. Just as Solokha shut the door after him, she heard another tap under the window. It was the Cossack Sverbygooze. As to this one, he decidedly could never have been hidden in a sack, for no sack large enough could ever have been found. In person he was even stouter than the elder, and as to height, he was even taller than Choop's kinsman. So Solokha went with him into the kitchen garden, in order to hear whatever he had to say to her.

The blacksmith looked vacantly round the room, listening at times to the songs of the carolling parties. His eyes rested at last on the sacks: "Why do these sacks lie here? They ought to have been taken away long ago. This stupid love has made quite a fool of me; to-morrow is a festival, and the room is still full of rubbish. I will clear it away into the smithy!" And the blacksmith went to the enormous sacks, tied them as tightly as he could, and would have lifted them on his shoulders; but it was evident that his thoughts were far away, otherwise he could not have helped hearing how Choop hissed when the cord with which the sack was tied twisted his hair, and how the stout elder began to hiccup very distinctly. "Shall I never get this silly Oxana out of my head?" mused the blacksmith; "I will not think of her; and yet, in spite of myself, I think of her, and of her alone. How is it that thoughts come into one's head against one's own will? What, the devil! Why the sacks appear to have grown heavier than they were; it seems as if there was something else besides charcoal! What a fool I am! have I forgotten that everything seems to me heavier than it used to be? Some time ago, with one hand I could bend and unbend a copper coin, or a horse-shoe; and now, I cannot lift a few sacks of charcoal; soon every breath of wind will blow me off my legs. No," cried he, after having remained silent for a while, and coming to himself again, "shall it be said that I am a woman? No one shall have the laugh against me; had

I ten such sacks, I would lift them all at once." And, accordingly, he threw the sacks upon his shoulders, although two strong men could hardly have lifted them. "I will take this little one, too," continued he, taking hold of the little one, at the bottom of which was coiled up the devil. "I think I put my instruments into it"; and thus saying, he went out of the cottage, whistling the tune:

"No wife I'll have to bother me."

Songs and shouts grew louder and louder in the streets; the crowds of strolling people were increased by those who came in from the neighbouring villages; the lads gave way to their frolics and sports. Often amongst the Christmas carols might be heard a gay song, just improvised by some young Cossack. Hearty laughter rewarded the improviser. The little windows of the cottages flew open, and from them was thrown a sausage or a piece of pie, by the thin hand of some old woman or some aged peasant, who alone remained indoors. The booty was eagerly caught in the sacks of the young people. In one place, the lads formed a ring to surround a group of maidens; nothing was heard but shouts and screams; one was throwing a snowball, another was endeavouring to get hold of a sack crammed with Christmas donations. In another place, the girls caught hold of some youth, or put something in his way, and down he fell with his sack. It seemed as if the whole of the night would pass away in these festivities. And the night, as if on purpose, shone so brilliantly; the gleam of the snow made the beams of the moon still whiter.

The blacksmith with his sacks stopped suddenly. He fancied he heard the voice and the sonorous laughter of Oxana in the midst of a group of maidens. It thrilled through his whole frame; he threw the sacks on the ground with so much force that the clerk, sitting at the bottom of one of them, groaned with pain, and the elder hiccupped aloud; then, keeping only the little sack upon his shoulders, the blacksmith joined a company of lads who followed close after a group of maidens, amongst whom he thought he had heard Oxana's voice.

"Yes, indeed; there she is! standing like a queen, her dark eyes sparkling with pleasure! There is a handsome youth speaking with her; his speech seems very amusing, for she is laughing; but does she not always laugh?" Without knowing why he did it and as if against his will, the blacksmith pushed his way through the crowd, and stood beside her.

"Ah! Vakoola, here art thou; a good evening to thee!" said the belle, with the very smile which drove Vakoola quite mad. "Well, hast thou received much? Eh! what a small sack! And didst thou get the boots that the Tsarina wears? Get those boots and I'll marry thee!" and away she ran laughing with the crowd.

The blacksmith remained riveted to the spot. "No, I cannot; I have not the strength to endure it any longer," said he at last. "But, Heavens! why is she so beautiful? Her looks, her voice, all, all about her makes my blood boil! No, I cannot get the better of it; it is time to put an end to this. Let my soul perish! I'll go and drown myself, and then all will be over." He dashed forwards with hurried steps, overtook the group, approached Oxana, and said to her in a resolute voice: "Farewell, Oxana! Take whatever bridegroom thou pleasest; make a fool of whom thou wilt; as for me, thou shalt never more meet me in this world!" The beauty seemed astonished, and was about to speak, but the blacksmith waved his hand and ran away.

"Whither away, Vakoola?" cried the lads, seeing him run. "Farewell, brothers," answered the blacksmith. "God grant that we may meet in another world; but in this we meet no more! Fare you well! keep a kind remembrance of me. Pray Father Kondrat to say a mass for my sinful soul. Ask him forgiveness that I did not, on account of worldly cares, paint the tapers for the church. Everything that is found in my big box I give to the Church; farewell!"—and thus saying, the blacksmith went on running, with his sack on his back.

"He has gone mad!" said the lads. "Poor lost soul!" piously ejaculated an old woman who happened to pass by; "I'll go and tell about the blacksmith having hanged himself."

Vakoola, after having run for some time along the streets, stopped to take breath. "Well, where am I running?" thought he; "is really all lost?—I'll try one thing more; I'll go to the fat Patzuck, the Zaporozhian. They say he knows every devil, and has the power of doing everything he wishes; I'll go to him; 'tis the same thing for the perdition of my soul." At this, the devil, who had long remained quiet and motionless, could not refrain from giving vent to his joy by leaping in the sack. But the blacksmith, thinking he had caught the sack with his hand, and thus occasioned the movement himself, gave a hard blow on the sack with his fist, and after shaking it about on his shoulders, went off to the fat Patzuck.

This fat Patzuck had indeed once been a Zaporozhian. Nobody, however, knew whether he had been turned out of that warlike community, or whether he had fled from it of his own accord. He had already been for some ten, nay, it might even be for some fifteen years, settled at Dikanka. At first, he had lived as best suited a Zaporozhian; working at nothing, sleeping three-quarters of the day, eating not less than would satisfy six harvest-men, and drinking almost a whole pailful at once. It must be allowed that there was plenty of room for food and drink in Patzuck; for, though he was not very tall, he tolerably made up for it in bulk. Moreover, the trousers he wore were so wide, that long as might be the strides he took in walking, his feet were never seen at all, and he might have been taken for a wine cask moving along the streets. This may have been the reason for giving him the nickname of "Fatty." A few weeks had hardly passed since his arrival·in the village, when it came to be known that he was a wizard. If anyone happened to fall ill, he called Patzuck directly; and Patzuck had only to mutter a few words to put an end to the illness at once. Had any hungry Cossack swallowed a fish-bone, Patzuck knew how to give him right skilfully a slap on the back, so that the fish-bone went where it ought to go without causing any pain to the Cossack's throat. Latterly, Patzuck was scarcely ever seen out of doors. This was perhaps caused by laziness, and perhaps, also, because to get through the door was a task which with every year grew more and more difficult for him. So the villagers were obliged to repair to his own lodgings whenever they wanted to consult him. The blacksmith opened the door, not without some fear. He saw Patzuck sitting on the floor after the Turkish fashion. Before him was a tub on which stood a tureen full of lumps of dough cooked in grease. The tureen was put, as if intentionally, on a level with his mouth. Without moving a single finger, he bent his head a little towards the tureen, and sipped the gravy, catching the lumps of dough with his teeth. "Well," thought Vakoola to himself, "this fellow is still lazier than Choop; Choop at least eats with a spoon, but this one does not even raise his hand!" Patzuck seemed to be busily engaged with his meal, for he took not the slightest notice of the entrance of the blacksmith, who, as soon as he crossed the threshold, made a low bow.

"I am come to thy worship, Patzuck!" said Vakoola, bowing once more. The fat Patzuck lifted his head and went on eating the lumps of dough.

"They say that thou art—I beg thy pardon," said the blacksmith, endeavouring to compose himself, "I do not say it to offend thee—that thou hast the devil among thy friends"; and in saying these words Vakoola was already afraid he had spoken too much to the point, and had not sufficiently softened the hard words he had used, and that Patzuck would throw at his head both the tub and the tureen; he even stepped a little on one side and covered his face with his sleeve, to prevent it from being sprinkled by the gravy.

But Patzuck looked up and continued sipping.

The encouraged blacksmith resolved to proceed:—"I am come to thee, Patzuck; God grant thee plenty of everything, and bread in good *proportion!*" The blacksmith knew how to put in a fashionable word sometimes; it was a talent he had acquired during his stay at Poltava, when he painted the centurion's palisade. "I am on the point of endangering the salvation of my sinful soul! nothing in this world can serve me! Come what will, I am resolved to seek the help of the devil. Well, Patzuck," said he, seeing that the other remained silent, "what am I to do?"

"If thou wantest the devil, go to the devil!" answered Patzuck, not giving him a single look, and going on with his meal.

"I am come to thee for this very reason," returned the blacksmith with a bow; "besides thyself, methinks there is hardly anybody in the world who knows how to go to the devil."

Patzuck, without saying a word, ate up all that remained on the dish. "Please, good man, do not refuse me!" urged the blacksmith. "And if there be any want of pork, or sausages, or buckwheat, or even linen or millet, or anything else—why, we know how honest folk manage these things. I shall not be stingy. Only do tell me, if it be only by a hint, how to find the way to the devil."

"He who has got the devil on his back has no great way to go to him," said Patzuck quietly, without changing his position.

Vakoola fixed his eyes upon him as if searching for the meaning of these words on his face. "What does he mean?" thought he, and opened his mouth as if to swallow his first word. But Patzuck kept silence. Here Vakoola noticed that there was no longer either tub or tureen before him, but instead of them there stood upon the floor two wooden pots, the one full of curd dumplings, the other full of sour cream. Involuntarily his thoughts and his eyes became riveted to these pots. "Well, now," thought he, "how will Patzuck eat the dumplings? He will not bend down to catch them like the bits of dough, and, moreover, it is impossible; for they ought to be first dipped into the cream." This thought had hardly crossed the mind of Vakoola, when Patzuck opened his mouth, looked at the dumplings, and then opened it still wider. Immediately, a dumpling jumped out of the pot, dipped itself into the cream, turned over on the other side, and went right into Patzuck's mouth. Patzuck ate it, once more opened his mouth, and in went another dumpling in the same way. All Patzuck had to do was to chew and to swallow them. "That is wondrous indeed," thought the blacksmith, and astonishment made him also open his mouth; but he felt directly, that a dumpling jumped into it also, and that his lips were already smeared with cream; he pushed it away, and after having wiped his lips, began to think about the marvels that happen in the world and the wonders one may work with the help of the devil; at the same time he felt more than ever convinced that Patzuck alone could help him. "I will beg of him still more earnestly to explain to me—but, what do I see? to-day is a fast, and he is eating dumplings, and dumplings are not food for fast days!¹ What a fool I am! staying here and giving way to temptation! Away, away," and the pious blacksmith ran with all speed out of the cottage. The devil, who remained all the while sitting in the sack, and already rejoiced at the glorious victim he had entrapped, could not endure to see him get free from his clutches. As soon as the blacksmith left the sack a little loose, he sprang out of it and sat upon the blacksmith's neck.

---

¹ Russians are much more severe in their fasts than Catholics, eating no milk or eggs. Some even go so far as to eat no fish and no hot dishes, restricting their food to cold boiled vegetables and bread.

Vakoola felt a cold shudder run through all his frame; his courage gave way, his face grew pale, he knew not what to do; he was already on the point of making the sign of the cross; but the devil, bending his dog's muzzle to his right ear, whispered: "Here I am, I, thy friend; I will do everything for a comrade and a friend such as thou! I'll give thee as much money as thou canst wish for!" squeaked he in his left ear. "No later than this very day Oxana shall be ours!" continued he, turning his muzzle once more to the right ear.

The blacksmith stood considering. "Well," said he, at length, "on this condition I am ready to be thine."

The devil clapped his hands and began to indulge his joy by springing about on the blacksmith's neck. "Now, I've caught him!" thought he to himself. "Now, I'll take my revenge upon thee, my dear fellow, for all thy paintings and all thy tales about devils! What will my fellows say when they come to know that the most pious man in the village is in my power?" and the devil laughed heartily at the thought of how he would tease all the long-tailed breed in hell, and how the lame devil, who was reputed the most cunning of them all for his tricks, would feel provoked.

"Well, Vakoola!" squeaked he, while he continued sitting on Vakoola's neck, as if fearing the blacksmith should escape; "thou knowest well that nothing can be done without contract."

"I am ready," said the blacksmith. "I've heard that it is the custom with you to write it in blood; well, stop, let me take a nail out of my pocket"—and putting his hand behind him, he suddenly seized the devil by his tail.

"Look, what fun!" cried the devil, laughing. "Well, let me alone now, there's enough of play!"

"Stop, my dear fellow!" cried the blacksmith, "What wilt thou say now?" and he made the sign of the cross. The devil grew as docile as a lamb. "Stop," continued the blacksmith, drawing him by the tail down to the ground; "I will teach thee how to make good men and upright Christians sin;" and the blacksmith sprang on his back, and once more raised his hand to make the sign of the cross.

"Have mercy upon me, Vakoola!" groaned the devil in a lamentable voice; "I am ready to do whatever thou wilt, only do not make the dread sign of the cross on me!"

"Ah! that is the strain thou singest now, cursed German that thou art! I know now what to do! Take me a ride on thy back directly, and harkee! a pretty ride must I have!"

"Whither?" gasped the mournful devil.

"To St. Petersburg, straightway to the Tsarina!" and the blacksmith thought he should faint with terror as he felt himself rising up in the air.

Oxana remained a long time pondering over the strange speech of the blacksmith. Something within her told her that she had behaved with too much cruelty towards him. "What if he should indeed resort to some frightful decision! May not such a thing be expected! He may, perhaps, fall in love with some other girl, and, out of spite, proclaim *her* to be the belle of the village! No, that he would not do, he is too much in love with me! I am so handsome! For none will he ever leave me. He is only joking; he only feigns. Ten minutes will not pass, ere he returns to look at me. I am indeed too harsh towards him. Why not let him have a kiss? just as if it were against my will; that to a certainty would make him quite delighted!" and the flighty belle began once more to sport with her friends. "Stop," said one of them, "the blacksmith has left his sacks behind; just see what enormous sacks too! His luck has been better than ours; methinks he has got whole quarters of mutton, and sausages, and loaves without number. Plenty indeed; one might feed upon the whole of next fortnight."

"Are these the blacksmith's sacks?" asked Oxana; "let us take them into my cottage just to see what he has got in them." All laughingly agreed to her proposal.

"But we shall never be able to lift them!" cried the girls, trying to move the sacks.

"Stay a bit," said Oxana; "come with me to fetch a sledge, and we'll drag them home on it."

The whole party ran to fetch a sledge.

The prisoners were far from pleased at sitting in the sacks, notwithstanding that the clerk had succeeded in poking a big hole with his finger. Had there been nobody near, he would perhaps have found the means of making his escape; but he could not endure the thought of creeping out of the sack before a whole crowd, and of being laughed at by everyone, so he resolved to await the event, giving only now and then a suppressed groan under the impolite boots of Choop. Choop had no less a desire to be set free, feeling that there was something lying under him, which was excessively inconvenient to sit upon. But on hearing his daughter's decision he remained quiet and no longer felt inclined to creep out, considering that he would have certainly some hundred, or perhaps even two hundred steps to walk to get to his dwelling; that upon creeping out, he would have his sheepskin coat to button, his belt to buckle—what a trouble! and last of all, that he had left his cap behind him at Solokha's. So he thought it better to wait till the maidens drew him home on a sledge.

The event, however, proved to be quite contrary to his expectations; at the same time that the maidens ran to bring the sledge, Choop's kinsman left the vodka-shop, very cross and dejected. The mistress of the shop would on no account give him credit; he had resolved to wait until some kind-hearted Cossack should step in and offer him a glass of vodka; but, as if purposely, all the Cossacks remained at home, and as became good Christians, ate *kootia* with their families. Thinking about the corruption of manners, and about the Jewish mistress of the shop having a wooden heart, the kinsman went straight to the sacks and stopped in amazement. "What sacks are these? somebody has left them on the

road," said he, looking round. "There must be pork for a
certainty in them! Who can it be? who has had the good
luck to get so many donations? Were there nothing more
than buckwheat cakes and millet-biscuits—why, that would
be well enough! But supposing there were only loaves, well,
they are welcome too! The Jewess gives a glass of vodka for
every loaf. I had better bring them out of the way at once,
lest anybody should see them!" and he lifted on his shoulders
the sack in which sat Choop and the clerk, but feeling it to be
too heavy, "No," said he, "I could not carry it home alone.
Now, here comes, as if purposely, the weaver, Shapoovalenko!
Good-evening, Ostap!"

"Good-evening," said the weaver, stopping.

"Where art thou going?"

"I am walking without any purpose, just where my legs
carry me."

"Well, my good man, help me to carry off these sacks; some
caroller has left them here in the midst of the road. We will
divide the booty between us."

"And what is there in the sacks? rolls or loaves?"

"Plenty of everything, I should think." And both hastily
snatched sticks out of a palisade, laid one of the sacks upon
them, and carried it away on their shoulders.

"Where shall we carry it? to the vodka-shop?" asked the
weaver, leading the way.

"I thought, too, of carrying it there; but the vile Jewess will
not give us credit; she will think we have stolen it somewhere,
the more so that I have just left her shop. We had better
carry it to my cottage. Nobody will interfere with us; my
wife is not at home."

"Art thou sure that she is not at home?" asked the weaver
warily.

"Thank Heaven, I am not yet out of my mind," answered
the kinsman. "What should I do there if she were at home?
I expect she will wander about all night with the rest of the
women."

"Who is there?" cried the kinsman's wife, hearing the noise which the two friends made in coming into the passage with the sack.

The kinsman was quite aghast.

"What now?" muttered the weaver, letting his arms drop.

The kinsman's wife was one of those treasures which are often found in this good world of ours. Like her husband, she scarcely ever remained at home, but went all day long fawning among wealthy, gossiping old women; paid them different compliments, ate their donations with great appetite, and beat her husband only in the morning, because it was the only time that she saw him. Their cottage was even older than the trousers of the village scribe. Many holes in the roof remained uncovered and without thatch; of the palisade round the house, few sticks existed, for no one who was going out ever took with him a stick to drive away the dogs, but went round by the kinsman's kitchen garden and got one out of his palisade. Sometimes no fire was lighted in the cottage for three days together. Everything which the affectionate wife succeeded in obtaining from kind people was hidden by her as far as possible out of the reach of her husband; and if he had got anything which he had not had the time to sell at the vodka-shop, she invariably snatched it from him. However meek the kinsman's temper might be, he did not like to yield to her at once; for which reason, he generally left the house with black eyes, and his dear better-half went moaning to tell stories to the old women about the ill conduct of her husband, and the blows she had received at his hands.

Now, it is easy to understand the displeasure of the weaver and the kinsman at her sudden appearance. Putting the sack on the ground, they took up a position of defence in front of it, and covered it with the wide skirts of their coats; but it was already too late. The kinsman's wife, although her old eyes had grown dim, saw the sack at once. "That's good," she

said, with the countenance of a hawk at the sight of its prey;
"that's good of you to have collected so much. That's the
way good people always behave! But it cannot be! I think
you must have stolen it somewhere; show me directly what
you have got there!—show me the sack directly! Do you
hear me?"

"May the bald devil show it to thee! we will not," answered
the kinsman, assuming an air of dogged resolution.

"Why should we?" said the weaver; "the sack is ours, not
thine."

"Thou shalt show it to me, thou good-for-nothing drunkard,"
said she, giving the tall kinsman a blow under his chin, and
pushing her way to the sack. The kinsman and the weaver,
however, stood her attack courageously, and drove her back;
but had hardly time to recover themselves, when the woman
darted once more into the passage, this time with a poker
in her hand. In no time she gave a cut over her husband's
fingers, another on the weaver's hand, and stood beside the
sack.

"Why did we let her go?" said the weaver, coming to his
senses.

"Why did we indeed? and why didst thou?" said the
kinsman.

"Your poker seems to be an iron one!" said the weaver,
after keeping silent for a while, and scratching his back.
"My wife bought one at the fair last year; well, hers is not to
be compared—does not hurt at all."

The triumphant dame, in the meanwhile, set her candle on
the floor, opened the sack, and looked into it.

But her old eyes, which had so quickly caught sight of the
sack, for this time deceived her. "Why, here lies a whole
boar!" cried she, clapping her hands with delight.

"A boar, a whole boar! dost hear?" said the weaver, giving
the kinsman a push. "And thou alone art to blame."

"What's to be done?" muttered the kinsman, shrugging his
shoulders.

"How, what? why are we standing here quietly? we must have the sack back again! Come!"

"Away, away with thee! it is our boar!" cried the weaver, advancing.

"Away, away with thee, she-devil! it is not thy property," said the kinsman.

The old hag once more took up the poker, but at the same moment Choop stepped out of the sack, and stood in the middle of the passage stretching his limbs like a man just awake from a long sleep.

The kinsman's wife shrieked in terror, while the others opened their mouths in amazement.

"What did she say, then, the old fool—that it was a boar?"

"It's not a boar!" said the kinsman, straining his eyes.

"Just see, what a man someone has thrown into the sack," said the weaver, stepping back in a fright. "They may say what they will—the evil spirit must have lent his hand to the work; the man could never have gone through a window."

"'Tis my kinsman," cried the kinsman, after having looked at Choop.

"And who else should it be, then?" said Choop, laughing. "Was it not a capital trick of mine? And you thought of eating me like pork? Well, I'll give you good news: there is something lying at the bottom of the sack; if it be not a boar, it must be a sucking-pig, or something of the sort. All the time there was something moving under me."

The weaver and the kinsman rushed to the sack, the wife caught hold of it on the other side, and the fight would have been renewed, had not the clerk, who saw no escape left, crept out of the sack.

The kinsman's wife, quite stupefied, let go the clerk's leg, which she had taken told of in order to drag him out of the sack.

"There's another one!" cried the weaver with terror; "the

devil knows what happens now in the world—it's enough to send one mad. No more sausages or loaves—men are thrown into the sacks."

"'Tis the devil!" muttered Choop, more astonished than anyone. "Well, now, Solokha!—and to put the clerk in a sack too! That is why I saw her room all full of sacks. Now, I have it: she has got two men in each of them; and I thought that I was the only one. Well now, Solokha!"

The maidens were somewhat astonished at finding only one sack left. "There is nothing to be done; we must content ourselves with this one," said Oxana. They all went at once to the sack, and succeeded in lifting it upon the sledge. The elder resolved to keep quiet, considering that if he cried out, and asked them to undo the sack, and let him out, the stupid girls would run away, fearing they had got the devil in the sack, and he would be left in the street till the next morning. Meanwhile, the maidens, with one accord, taking one another by the hand, flew like the wind with the sledge over the crisp snow. Many of them, for fun, sat down upon the sledge; some went right upon the elder's head. But he was determined to bear everything. At last they reached Oxana's house, opened the doors of the passage and of the room, and with shouts of laughter brought in the sack. "Let us see what we have got here," cried they, and hastily began to undo the sack. At this juncture, the hiccups of the elder (which had not ceased for a moment all the time he had been sitting in the sack) increased to such a degree that he could not refrain from giving vent to them in the loudest key. "Ah! there is somebody in the sack!" shrieked the maidens, and they darted in a fright towards the door.

"What does this mean?" said Choop, stepping in. "Where are you rushing, like mad things?"

"Ah! father," answered Oxana, "there is somebody sitting in the sack!"

"In what sack? Where did you get this sack from?"

"The blacksmith threw it down in the middle of the road," was the answer.

"I thought as much!" muttered Choop. "Well, what are you afraid of, then? Let us see. Well, my good man (excuse me for not calling thee by thy Christian and surname), please to make thy way out of the sack."

The elder came out.

"Lord have mercy upon us!" cried the maidens.

"The elder was in too!" thought Choop to himself, looking at him from head to foot, as if not trusting his eyes. "There now! Eh!" and he could say no more. The elder felt no less confused, and he knew not what to say. "It seems to be rather cold out of doors?" asked he, turning to Choop.

"Yes! the frost is rather severe," answered Choop. "Do tell me, what dost thou use to black thy boots with: tallow or tar?" He did not at all wish to put this question; he intended to ask—How didst thou come to be in this sack? but he knew not himself how it was that his tongue asked quite another question.

"I prefer tar," answered the elder. "Well, good-bye, Choop," said he, and putting his cap on, he stepped out of the room.

"What a fool I was to ask him what he uses to black his boots with," muttered Choop, looking at the door out of which the elder had just gone. "Well, Solokha! To put such a man into a sack! May the devil take her; and I, fool that I was—but where is that infernal sack?"

"I threw it into the corner," said Oxana, "there is nothing more in it."

"I know these tricks well! Nothing in it, indeed! Give it me directly; there must be one more! Shake it well. Is there nobody? Abominable woman! And yet to look at her one would think she must be a saint, that she never had a sin——"

But let us leave Choop giving vent to his anger, and return

to the blacksmith; the more so as time is running away, and
by the clock it must be near nine.

At first, Vakoola could not help feeling afraid at rising to
such a height that he could distinguish nothing upon the
earth, and at coming so near the moon, that if he had not
bent down, he would certainly have touched it with his cap.
Yet, after a time, he recovered his presence of mind, and
began to laugh at the devil. All was bright in the sky. A
light silvery mist covered the transparent air. Everything
was distinctly visible; and the blacksmith even noticed how
a wizard flew past him, sitting in a pot; how some stars,
gathered in a group, played at blind man's buff; how a whole
swarm of spirits were whirling about in the distance; how a
devil who danced in the moonbeam, seeing him riding, took
off his cap and made him a bow; how there was a besom
flying, on which, apparently, a witch had just taken a ride.
They met many other things; and all, on seeing the blacksmith, stopped for a moment to look at him, and then continued their flight far away. The blacksmith went on flying,
and suddenly he saw St. Petersburg all in a blaze. (There
must have been an illumination that day.) Flying past the
town gate, the devil changed into a horse, and the blacksmith saw himself riding a high-stepping steed, in the middle
of the street. "Good heavens! What a noise, what a clatter,
what a blaze!" On either side rose houses, several stories
high; from every quarter the clatter of horses' hoofs, and of
wheels arose, like thunder; at every step arose tall houses, as
if starting from beneath the ground; bridges quivered under
flying carriages; the coachmen shouted; the snow crisped
under thousands of sledges rushing in every direction;
pedestrians kept the wall of the houses along the footpath,
all studded with flaring pots of fire, and their gigantic
shadows danced upon the walls, losing themselves amongst
the chimneys and on the roofs. The blacksmith looked with
amazement on every side. It seemed to him as if all the houses

5

looked at him with their innumerable fire-eyes. He saw such a number of gentlemen wearing fur cloaks covered with cloth, that he no longer knew to which of them he ought to take off his cap. "Gracious Lord! What a number of nobility one sees here!" thought the blacksmith; "I suppose everyone here, who goes in a fur cloak, can be no less than a magistrate! and as for the persons who sit in those wonderful carts with glasses, they must be, if not the chiefs of the town, certainly commissaries, and, maybe, of a still higher rank!"

Here, the devil put an end to his reflections, by asking if he was to bring him right before the Tsarina? "No, I should be too afraid to go at once," answered the blacksmith; "but I know there must be some Zaporozhians here, who passed through Dikanka last autumn on their way to Petersburg. They were going on business to the Tsarina. Let us have their advice. Now, devil, get into my pocket, and bring me to those Zaporozhians." In less than a minute the devil grew so thin and so small that he had no trouble in getting into the pocket, and in the twinkling of an eye, Vakoola (himself, he knew not how) ascended a staircase, opened a door and fell a little back, struck by the rich furniture of a spacious room. Yet he felt a little more at ease when he recognised the same Zaporozhians who had passed through Dikanka. They were sitting upon silk-covered sofas, with their tar-be-smeared boots tucked under them, and were smoking the strongest tobacco fibres.

"Good-evening, God help you, your worships!" said the blacksmith, coming nearer, and he made a low bow, almost touching the ground with his forehead.

"Who is that?" asked a Zaporozhian, who sat near Vakoola, of another who was sitting farther off.

"Do you not recognise me at once?" said Vakoola; "I am the blacksmith, Vakoola! Last autumn, as you passed through Dikanka, you remained nearly two days at my cottage. God grant you good health, and many happy

41

years! It was I who put a new iron tyre round one of the forewheels of your vehicle."

"Ah!" said the same Zaporozhian, "it is the blacksmith who paints so well. Good-evening, countryman, what didst thou come for?"

"Only just to look about. They say——"

"Well, my good fellow," said the Zaporozhian, assuming a grand air, and trying to speak with the high Russian accent, "what dost thou think of the town? Is it large?"

The blacksmith was no less desirous to show that he also understood good manners. We have already seen that he knew something of fashionable language. "The site is quite considerable," answered he very composedly. "The houses are enormously big, the paintings they are adorned with are thoroughly important. Some of the houses are to an extremity ornamented with gold letters. No one can say a word to the contrary: the proportion is marvellous!" The Zaporozhians, hearing the blacksmith so familiar with fine language, drew a conclusion very much to his advantage.

"We will have a chat with thee presently, my dear fellow. Now, we must go at once to the Tsarina."

"To the Tsarina? Be kind, your worships, take me with you!"

"Take thee with us?" said the Zaporozhian, with an expression such as a tutor would assume towards a boy four years old, who begs to ride on a real, live, great horse. "What hast thou to do there? No, it cannot be," and his features took an important look. "My dear fellow, we have to speak to the Tsarina on business."

"Do take me," urged the blacksmith. "Beg!" whispered he to the devil, striking his pocket with his fist. Scarcely had he done so, when another Zaporozhian said, "Well, come, comrades, we will take him."

"Well, then, let him come!" said the others.

"Put on such a dress as ours, then."

The blacksmith hastily donned a green dress, when the

door opened, and a man, in a coat all ornamented with silver braid, came in and said it was time to start.

Once more was the blacksmith overwhelmed with astonishment, as he rolled along in an enormous carriage, hung on springs, lofty houses seeming to run away on both sides of him, and the pavement to roll of its own accord under the feet of the horses.

"Gracious Lord! what a glare," thought the blacksmith to himself. "We have no such light at Dikanka, even during the day." The Zaporozhians entered, stepped into a magnificent hall, and went up a brilliantly lighted staircase. "What a staircase!" thought the blacksmith; "it is a pity to walk upon it. What ornaments! And they say that fairy-tales are so many lies; they are plain truth! My heavens! what a balustrade! what workmanship! The iron alone must have cost not less than some fifty roubles!"

Having ascended the staircase, the Zaporozhians passed through the first hall. Warily did the blacksmith follow them, fearing at every step to slip on the waxed floor. They passed three more saloons, and the blacksmith had not yet recovered from his astonishment. Coming into a fourth, he could not refrain from stopping before a picture which hung on the wall. It represented the Holy Virgin, with the Infant Jesus in her arms. "What a picture! what beautiful painting!" thought he. "She seems to speak, she seems to be alive! And the Holy Infant! there, he stretches out his little hands! there, it laughs, the poor babe! And what colours! Good heavens! what colours! I should think there was no ochre used in the painting; certainly nothing but ultramarine and lake! And what a brilliant blue! Capital workmanship! The background must have been done with white lead! And yet," he continued, stepping to the door and taking the handle in his hand, "however beautiful these paintings may be, this brass handle is still more worthy of admiration; what neat work! I should think all this must have been made by German blacksmiths at the most exorbitant prices." . . .

The blacksmith might have gone on for a long time with his reflections, had not the attendant in the braid-covered dress given him a push, telling him not to remain behind the others. The Zaporozhians passed two rooms more, and stopped. Some generals, in gold-embroidered uniforms, were waiting there. The Zaporozhians bowed in every direction, and stood in a group. A minute afterwards there entered, attended by a numerous suite, a man of majestic stature, rather stout, dressed in the hetman's uniform and yellow boots. His hair was uncombed; one of his eyes had a small cataract on it; his face wore an expression of stately pride; his every movement gave proof that he was accustomed to command. All the generals, who before his arrival were strutting about somewhat haughtily in their gold-embroidered uniforms, came bustling towards him with profound bows, seeming to watch every one of his words, nay, of his movements, that they might run and see his desires fulfilled. The hetman did not pay any attention to all this, scarcely nodding his head, and went straight to the Zaporozhians.

They bowed to him with one accord till their brows touched the ground.

"Are all of you here?" asked he, in a somewhat drawling voice, with a slight nasal twang.

"Yes, father, every one of us is here," answered the Zaporozhains, bowing once more.

"Remember to speak just as I taught you."

"We will, father, we will!"

"Is it the Tsar?" asked the blacksmith of one of the Zaporozhians.

"The Tsar! a great deal more; it is Potemkin himself!" was the answer.

Voices were heard in the adjoining room, and the blacksmith knew not where to turn his eyes, when he saw a multitude of ladies enter, dressed in silk gowns with long trains, and courtiers in gold-embroidered coats and bag-wigs. He was dazzled with the glitter of gold, silver, and precious stones. The Zaporozhians fell with one accord on their knees, and cried with one voice, "Mother, have mercy upon us!" The blacksmith, too, followed their example, and stretched himself full length on the floor.

"Rise up!" was heard above their heads, in a commanding yet soft voice. Some of the courtiers officiously hastened to push the Zaporozhians forward.

"We will not arise, mother; we will die rather than arise!" cried the Zaporozhians.

Potemkin bit his lips. At last he came himself, and whispered imperatively to one of them. They arose. Then only did the blacksmith venture to raise his eyes, and saw before him a lady, not tall, somewhat stout, with powdered hair, blue eyes, and that majestic, smiling air which conquered everyone, and could be the attribute only of a sovereign lady.

"His Highness[1] promised to make me acquainted to-day with a people under my dominion whom I have not yet seen," said the blue-eyed lady, looking with curiosity at the Zaporozhians. "Are you satisfied with the manner in which you are provided for here?" asked she, coming nearer.

"Thank thee, mother! Provisions are good, though mutton is not quite so fine here as at home; but why should one be so very particular about it?"

Potemkin frowned at hearing them speak in quite a different manner from what he had told them to do.

One of the Zaporozhians stepped out from the group, and, in a dignified manner, began the following speech:—"Mother, have mercy upon us! What have we, thy faithful people, done to deserve thine anger? Have we ever given assistance to the miscreant Tartars? Did we ever help the Turks in anything? Have we betrayed thee in our acts, nay, even in our thoughts? Wherefore, then, art thou ungracious towards us? At first they told us thou hadst ordered fortresses

[1]Potemkin was created by Catherine II Prince of Tauride, with the title of Highness, an honour rarely bestowed in Russia.

to be raised against us; then we were told thou wouldst make regular regiments of us; now, we hear of new evils coming on us. In what were the Zaporozhians ever in fault with regard to thee? Was it in bringing thy army across Perekop? or in helping thy generals to get the better of the Crimean Tartars?"

Potemkin remained silent, and, with an unconcerned air, was brushing the diamonds which sparkled on his fingers.

"What do you ask for, then?" demanded Catherine, in a solicitous tone of voice.

The Zaporozhians looked knowingly at one another.

"Now's the time! the Tsarina asks what we want!" thought the blacksmith, and suddenly down he went on his knees. "Imperial Majesty! Do not show me thy anger, show me thy mercy! Let me know (and let not my question bring the wrath of thy Majesty's worship upon me!) of what stuff are made the boots that thou wearest on thy feet? I think there is no bootmaker in any country in the world who ever will be able to make such pretty ones. Gracious Lord! if ever my wife had such boots to wear!"

The empress laughed; the courtiers laughed too. Potemkin frowned and smiled at the same time. The Zaporozhians pushed the blacksmith, thinking he had gone mad.

"Stand up!" said the empress, kindly. "If thou wishest to have such shoes, thy wish may be easily fulfilled. Let him have directly my richest gold-embroidered shoes. This artlessness pleases me exceedingly." Then, turning towards a gentleman with a round pale face, who stood a little apart from the rest, and whose plain dress, with mother-of-pearl buttons, showed at once that he was not a courtier, "There you have," continued she, "a subject worthy of your witty pen."

"Your Imperial Majesty is too gracious! It would require a pen no less able than that of a Lafontaine!" answered, with a bow, the gentleman in the plain dress.

"Upon my honour! I tell you I am still under the impres-

sion of your '*Brigadier*.'[1] You read exceedingly well!"
Then, speaking once more to the Zaporoghians, she said, "I
was told that you never married at your Siecha?"

"How could that be, mother? Thou knowest well, by thyself, that no man could ever do without a woman," answered
the same Zaporozhian who had conversed with the blacksmith; and the blacksmith was astonished to hear one so well
acquainted with polished language speak to the Tsarina, as
if on purpose, in the coarsest accent used among peasants.

"A cunning people," thought he to himself; "he does it
certainly for some reason."

"We are no monks," continued the speaker, "we are sinful
men. Every one of us is as much inclined to forbidden fruit
as a good Christian can be. There are not a few among us
who have wives, only their wives do not live in the Siecha.
Many have their wives in Poland; others have wives in
Ukraine; there are some, too, who have wives in Turkey."

At this moment the shoes were brought to the blacksmith.

"Gracious Lord! what ornaments!" cried he, overpowered
with joy, grasping the shoes. "Imperial Majesty! if thou dost
wear such shoes upon thy feet (and thy Honour, I dare say,
does use them even for walking in the snow and the mud),
what, then, must thy feet be like?—whiter than sugar, at the
least, I should think!"

The empress, who really had charming feet of an exquisite
shape, could not refrain from smiling at such a compliment
from a simple-minded blacksmith, who, notwithstanding his
sunburnt features, must have been accounted a handsome
lad in his Zaporozhian dress.

The blacksmith, encouraged by the condescension of the
Tsarina, was already on the point of asking her some ques-
tions about all sorts of things, whether it was true that

[1] The author alluded to is Von Wiessen, who, in his writings (particularly
in two comedies, the *Brigadier*, and the *Young Nobleman without Employ-
ment*), ridiculed the then prevailing fashion amongst the Russian nobility
of despising national and blindly following foreign (particularly French)
customs.

sovereigns fed upon nothing but honey and lard, and so on; but feeling the Zaporozhians pull the skirts of his coat, he resolved to keep silent; and when the empress turned to the older Cossacks, and began to ask them about their way of living, and their manners, in the Siecha, he stepped a little back, bent his head towards his pocket, and said in a low voice: "Quick, carry me hence, away!" and in no time he had left the town gate far behind.

"He is drowned! I'll swear to it, he's drowned! May I never leave this spot alive if he is not drowned!" said the fat weaver's wife, standing in the middle of the street, amidst a group of the villagers' wives.

"Then I am a liar? Did I ever steal anything? Did I ever cast an evil eye upon anyone, that I am no longer worthy of belief?" shrieked a hag wearing a Cossack's dress, and with a violet-coloured nose, brandishing her hands in the most violent manner. "May I never have another drink of water if old Pereperchenko's wife did not see with her own eyes how that the blacksmith has hanged himself!"

"The blacksmith hanged himself? what is this I hear?" said the elder, stepping out of Choop's cottage; and he pushed his way nearer to the talking women.

"Say rather, mayest thou never wish to drink vodka again, old drunkard!" answered the weaver's wife. "One must be as mad as thou art to hang one's self. He is drowned! drowned in the ice-hole! This I know as well as that thou just now didst come from the vodka-shop!"

"Shameless creature! what meanest thou to reproach me with?" angrily retorted the hag with the violet-coloured nose, "thou hadst better hold thy tongue, good-for-nothing woman Don't I know that the clerk comes every evening to thee?"

The weaver's wife became red in the face. "What does the clerk do? to whom does the clerk come? What lie art thou telling?"

"The clerk?" cried, in shrill voice, the clerk's wife, who,

dressed in a hare-skin cloak covered with blue nankeen, pushed her way towards the quarrelling ones; "I will let you know about the clerk! Who is talking here about the clerk?"

"There is she to whom the clerk pays his visits!" said the violet-nosed woman, pointing to the weaver's wife.

"So, thou art the witch," continued the clerk's wife, stepping nearer the weaver's wife; "thou art the witch who sends him out of his senses and gives him a charmed beverage in order to bewitch him?"

"Wilt thou leave me alone, she-devil!" cried the weaver's wife, drawing back.

"Cursed witch! Mayest thou never see thy children again, good-for-nothing woman!" and the clerk's wife spat right into the eyes of the weaver's wife.

The weaver's wife wished to return her the same compliment, but instead of that, spat on the unshaven beard of the elder, who had come near the squabblers in order to hear what was going on. "Ah! nasty creature!" cried the elder, wiping his face with his skirt, and lifting his whip. This motion made them all fly in different directions, scolding the whole time. "The abominable creature!" continued the elder, still wiping his beard. "So the blacksmith is drowned! Gracious Heaven! and such a capital painter! and what strong knives, and sickles, and ploughshares he used to forge! How strong he was himself!

"Yes," continued he, meditatively, "there are few such men in our village! That was the reason of the poor fellow's ill-temper, which I noticed while I was sitting in that confounded sack! So much for the blacksmith! He was here, and now nothing is left of him! And I was thinking of letting him shoe my speckled mare," . . . and, full of such Christian thoughts, the elder slowly went to his cottage.

Oxana was very downcast at hearing the news; she did not put any faith in the evidence of Pereperchenko's wife, or in the gossiping of the women. She knew the blacksmith to be too pious to venture on letting his soul perish. But what if indeed he had left the village with the resolve never to return? And scarcely could there be found anywhere such an accomplished lad as the blacksmith. And he loved her so intensely! He had endured her caprices longer than anyone else. All the night long, the belle turned beneath her cover-let, from right to left, and from left to right, and could not go to sleep. Now she scolded herself almost aloud, throwing herself into the most bewitching attitudes, which the dark-ness of the night hid even from herself; then, in silence, she resolved to think no more of anything and still continued thinking, and was burning with fever; and in the morning she was quite in love with the blacksmith.

Choop was neither grieved nor rejoiced at the fate of Vakoola; all his ideas had concentrated themselves into one: he could not for a moment forget Solokha's want of faith; and even when asleep, ceased not to abuse her.

The morning came; the church was crowded even before daylight. The elderly women, in their white linen veils, their flowing robes, and long jackets made of white cloth, piously made the sign of the cross, standing close to the entrance of the church. The Cossacks' wives, in green and yellow bodices, and some of them even in blue dresses, with gold braidings behind, stood a little before them. The girls endeavoured to get still nearer to the altar, and displayed whole shopfuls of ribbons on their heads, and of necklaces, little crosses, and silver coins on their necks. But right in front stood the Cossacks and the peasants, with their moustaches, their crown-tufts, their thick necks and their freshly-shaven chins, dressed for the most part in cloaks with hoods, from beneath which were seen white, and sometimes blue coats. On every face, wherever one looked, one might see it was a holiday. The elder already licked his lips at the idea of breaking his fast with a sausage. The girls were thinking about the pleasure of running about with the lads, and sliding upon the ice. The old women muttered their prayers more zeal-ously than ever. The whole church resounded with the thumps which the Cossack Sverbygooze gave with his fore-head against the floor as he prostrated himself.

Oxana alone was out of sorts. She said her prayers, and yet could not pray. Her heart was besieged by so many different feelings, one more mournful than the other, one more perplexing than the other, that the greatest dejection appeared upon her features, and tears moistened her eyes. None of the girls could understand the reason of her state, and none would have suspected its being occasioned by the blacksmith. And yet Oxana was not the only one who noticed his absence; the whole congregation remarked that there lacked something to the fullness of the festival. Moreover, the clerk, during his journey in the sack, had got a bad cold, and his cracked voice was hardly audible. The newly-arrived chanter had a deep bass indeed. But at all events it would have been much better if the blacksmith had been there, as he had so fine a voice, and knew how to chant the tunes which were used at Poltava; and besides, he was church-warden.

The matins were said. The liturgy had also been brought to a close. Well, what had indeed happened to the blacksmith?

The devil, with the blacksmith on his back, had flown with still greater speed during the remainder of the night. Vakoola soon reached his cottage. At the very moment he heard the crow of a cock. "Whither away?" cried he, seeing the devil in the act of sneaking off; and he caught him by his tail. "Wait a bit, my dear fellow; I have not done with thee; thou must get thy reward!" and, taking a stick, he gave him three blows across his back, so that the poor devil took to his heels, exactly as a peasant might do who had just been punished by a police officer. So, the enemy of mankind, instead of cheating, seducing, or leading anybody into foolishness, was made a fool of himself. After this, Vakoola went into the passage, buried himself in the hay, and slept till noon.

When he awoke, he was alarmed at seeing the sun high in the heavens. "I have missed matins and liturgy!" and the pious blacksmith fell into mournful thoughts, and decided that the sleep which had prevented him from going to church on such a festival was certainly a punishment inflicted by God for his sinful intention of killing himself. But he soon quieted his mind by resolving to confess no later than next week, and from that very day to make fifty genuflexions during his prayers for a whole year. Then he went into the room, but nobody was there; Solokha had not yet returned home. He cautiously drew the shoes from his breast pocket, and once more admired their beautiful workmanship, and marvelled at the events of the preceding night. Then he washed, and dressed himself as fine as he could, putting on the same suit of clothes which he had got from the Zaporozhians, took out of his box a new cap with a blue crown and a trimming of black sheepskin, which had never been worn since he bought it in Poltava; he took out also a new belt, of divers brilliant colours; wrapped up these with a scourge, in a handkerchief, and went straight to Choop's cottage.

Choop opened wide his eyes as he saw the blacksmith enter his room. He knew not at what most to marvel, whether at the blacksmith being once more alive, or at his having ventured to come into his house, or at his being dressed so finely, like a Zaporozhian; but he was still more astonished when he saw Vakoola undo his handkerchief, and set before him an entirely new cap, and such a belt as had never before been seen in the village; and when Vakoola fell at his knees, saying in a deprecating voice: "Father, have mercy on me! do not be angry with me! There, take this scourge, whip me as much as thou wilt! I give myself up. I acknowledge all my trespasses. Whip me, but put away thine anger! The more so that thou and my late father were like two brothers, and shared bread, and salt, and brandy together."

Choop could not help feeling inwardly pleased at seeing at

his feet the blacksmith, the very same blacksmith who would not concede a step to anyone in the village, and who bent copper coins between his fingers as if they were so many buckwheat fritters. To make himself still more important, Choop took the scourge, gave three strokes with it upon the blacksmith's back, and then said: "Well, that will do! Stand up! Attend to men older than thyself. I forget all that has taken place between us. Now, speak out, what dost thou want?"

"Father, let me have Oxana!"

Choop remained thinking for a while; he looked at the cap —he looked at the belt; the cap was beautiful—the belt not less so; he remembered the bad faith of Solokha, and said, in a resolute voice, "Well, send me thy marriage sponsors."

"Ah!" shrieked Oxana, stepping across the threshold; and she stared at him with a look of joy and astonishment.

"Look at the boots I have brought thee!" said Vakoola; "they are the very boots which the Tsarina wears."

"No, no, I do not want the boots!" said Oxana, and she waved her hands, never taking her eyes off him; "it will do without the boots." She could speak no more, and her face turned all crimson.

The blacksmith came nearer, and took her hand. The belle cast down her eyes. Never yet had she been so marvellously handsome; the exulting blacksmith gently stole a kiss, and her face flushed still redder, and she looked still prettier.

As the late archbishop happened to pass on a journey through Dikanka, he greatly commended the spot on which that village stands, and driving down the street, stopped his carriage before a new cottage. "Whose cottage is this, so highly painted?" asked his Eminence of a handsome woman who was standing before the gate, with an infant in her arms.

"It is the blacksmith Vakoola's cottage!" answered Oxana, for she it was, making him a deep curtsy.

"Very good painting, indeed! Capital painting!" said the

Right Eminent, looking at the door and the windows. And, in truth, every window was surrounded by a stripe of red paint; and the door was painted all over with Cossacks on horseback, with pipes in their mouths. But the archbishop bestowed still more praises on Vakoola, when he was made acquainted with the blacksmith's having performed public penance, and with his having painted, at his own expense, the whole of the church choir, green, with red flowers running over it. But Vakoola had done still more: he had painted the devil in hell, upon the wall which is to your left when you step into the church. This devil had such an odious face that no one could refrain from spitting, as they passed by. The women, as soon as their children began to cry, brought them to this picture and said, "Look! is he not an odious creature?" and the children stopped their tears, looked sideways at the picture, and clung more closely to their mother's bosom.

9 781473 318823